CORI DOERRFELD
Wild Baby

HARPER
An Imprint of HarperCollinsPublishers

To all families living in the wild

Wild Baby
Copyright © 2019 by Cori Doerrfeld
All rights reserved. Manufactured in China.
No part of this book may be used or reproduced in any manner whatsoever
without written permission except in the case of brief quotations embodied in critical
articles and reviews. For information address HarperCollins Children's Books,
a division of HarperCollins Publishers, 195 Broadway, New York, NY 10007.
www.harpercollinschildrens.com

Library of Congress Control Number: 2018938259
ISBN 978-0-06-269894-0
The artist used digital ink to create the illustrations for this book.
Book design by Alison Donalty and Michelle Cunningham
18 19 20 21 22   SCP   10 9 8 7 6 5 4 3 2 1
❖ First Edition

Wild stretch. Wild yawn.
Wild morning starts at dawn.

Wild jump. Wild free.

"Wild baby, wait for me!"

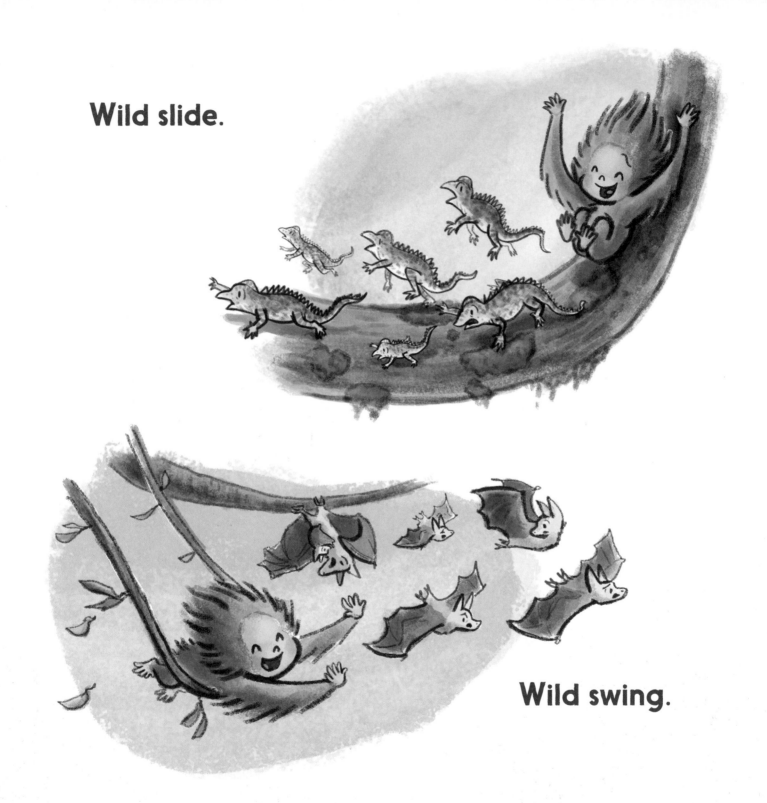

Wild slide.

Wild swing.

Wild hands
on everything!

Wild dance.

Wild hop.

Wild climb up to the top!

Wild find. Wild fun.

Wild baby on the run!

Wild path.
Wild pace.

Wild, crazy jungle chase!

Wild search.

Wild track.

"Wild baby, come right back!"

Wild danger! Wild trap!
Wild teeth about to . . .

Wild peek.

Wild frown.

Wild time to climb on down.

Wild trouble.

Wild drama.

Wild scolds from
wild mama.

Wild reason.
Wild story.

Wild baby says, "I'm sorry."

Wild smile.
Wild sighs.

"Wild mama,
close your eyes."

Wild gift?

Wild view!

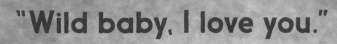

"Wild baby, I love you."